Book Club Edition

WALT DISNEY PRODUCTIONS

presents

BRER RABBIT
AND THE
POT OF GOLD

Random House 🏠 New York

One day Brer Bear and Brer Fox came walking down the road.

They saw Brer Rabbit standing outside his home in the brier patch.

Brer Rabbit saw them too, but he didn't let on.

He started to hatch a plan.

Brer Bear and Brer Fox were always trying
to catch Brer Rabbit.
They liked nothing better than rabbit stew.
But today Brer Rabbit was acting strange.

Brer Rabbit was busy drawing lines
in the dirt.

He pretended that he did not see
Brer Bear and Brer Fox watching him.

"Morning, Brer Rabbit," said Brer Bear.
"Fine day we are having," said Brer Fox.
"Oh! Uh, morning," said Brer Rabbit.
He acted very surprised.

"What are you drawing, Brer Rabbit?"
asked Brer Bear.

"Oh, I'm just planning a new home
for myself," said Brer Rabbit.

Brer Fox looked hard at the drawing.

He scratched his head.
"Looks mighty big,"
he said.

"No, it's just
right," said
Brer Rabbit.

"Twelve or fourteen rooms and a swimming pool," said Brer Rabbit.

"Twelve rooms? A swimming pool?" said Brer Fox.

"What will you use for money?" asked
Brer Bear and Brer Fox.

"Money? No problem!"
said Brer Rabbit. "I've
got plenty."

Then Brer Rabbit
ran for his doorway.

Brer Bear and Brer Fox took off after him.

Brer Rabbit did
not get far.

Brer Bear and Brer Fox marched him
over to a big tree.

Soon Brer Rabbit was tied up.
He pretended to be scared.

Brer Bear began to pick up sticks.
"Let's make a good hot cooking fire
and have some lunch," he said.

"Good idea, Brer Bear," said Brer Fox.
"But first we must get Brer Rabbit's
money bags."

"Money bags?" said Brer Rabbit.
"Oh, you mean my pot of gold."

"Pot of gold!" cried Brer Bear. "Where is it?"

"Untie me and I will show you," said Brer Rabbit.

"No, sir!" said Brer Fox. "You just tell us where your gold is."

"Very well," said Brer Rabbit, and he
told them where to look in the deep wood.
Off went Brer Bear and Brer Fox,
happy as could be.

Brer Bear and Brer Fox came to a big hill.
They had to climb a steep path.
Soon Brer Bear was out of breath.

Brer Bear wanted to stop and rest.

"Do you want that pot of gold or don't you?" said Brer Fox.

"Oh, all right, I'll go on," said Brer Bear.

Brer Bear got to the top of the hill first.

Suddenly he slid into a deep hole!

"Where are you, Brer Bear?" called Brer Fox.

And he slipped into the hole too!

Brer Fox landed right on top of Brer Bear.
They were both in the middle of a prickly
brier patch.

"Ouch! That Brer Rabbit! Thought he could trick us!" said Brer Fox. "Let's go back and make him lead us to that pot of gold!"

They pulled free of the prickly briers.

Brer Bear and Brer Fox went back
to Brer Rabbit.
He was still tied to the tree.

"Hi-ho, Brer Bear and Brer Fox," called
Brer Rabbit. "Did you find my pot of gold?"
"It was too heavy for us to lift," said
Brer Fox. "We need you to help us carry it."

"If you say so," said Brer Rabbit.
"But better hurry. It will be dark soon.
Untie me and I will show you a shortcut."

So Brer Bear untied Brer Rabbit.

They set off down the path.
"I have to stop at my house a minute,"
said Brer Rabbit.

And he made a dive for his front door.
"Whoa, there!" said Brer Bear and
Brer Fox. "No tricks!"

"No tricks at all," said Brer Rabbit.
"We just need some things for getting
the gold."

So Brer Bear and Brer Fox let him go.

Brer Rabbit came back with a fishnet
on a long pole.

"A fishnet for digging up gold?" shouted
Brer Bear. "Brer Rabbit is crazy!"
"Have you got a better idea?" yelled
Brer Fox.

But it was no use quarreling.
Only Brer Rabbit knew where the gold was.
So they followed him.

"We're getting close," Brer Rabbit said
after a long walk through the woods.

At last they stopped at the edge of a pond.
The sky was dark and the moon was out.

In the middle of the pond was
a round golden glow.
"There's my gold," said Brer Rabbit.
"All you have to do is scoop it up."

Brer Bear reached out with the fishnet.
But the pole was not long enough.

"Crawl out on a tree," said Brer Rabbit.
"Then you can reach the gold."

So Brer Bear crawled out on a large branch.
Brer Fox crawled out after him.
Again Brer Bear reached out for the gold.

CRACK! went the branch.
Into the pond went Brer Bear and Brer Fox!

"There you are!" called Brer Rabbit.
"Now all you have to do is scoop up the gold!"

Brer Rabbit looked up at the sky.
"Thanks for your help, Mr. Moon," he said.

Then Brer Rabbit ran off lickety split
down the path and through the woods.

And he laughed all the way home!